For my husband Illya,

who has taught me patience,

inspired hope,

and encouraged me to reach for the clouds.

For ordering information, write or telephone:

BARNABY & COMPANY PUBLISHING AND PRODUCTIONS, L.L.C.

P.O. Box 3198

Nantucket, MA 02584

Tel: 508.228.5114

Fax: 508.325.0011

E-mail: barnaby@nantucket.net

Visit Barnaby's Web Site!

www.barnabybear.com

On a faraway land many miles out to sea,
There lives a young bear named Barnaby.
He is sweet and adorable and cuddly, too.
He may be a bear, but he's like me and you.

Now Barnaby's tree house is chipping and graying,
There is work to be done and no time for playing.
With paint brush in paw, Barnaby sets on his way,
A splash of bold color will soon brighten the day.

Barnaby's tree house was perched high in the branches of a giant oak tree. It was his special hideaway.

From up above the sunsets lasted longer,

the stars shined brighter,

and Barnaby could almost touch the clouds.

All year long Barnaby took great care of his tree house.

One Saturday morning after a long, hard winter,
Barnaby noticed that the paint on his
tree house was starting to chip.
It's time to paint my tree house,
he thought.

Barnaby ran to tell his dog, Baxter.

He ran to tell his friends.

And he ran to tell his parents.
"That's a big project," said Barnaby's father. "Today is a busy day at the market. I'll help you tomorrow."

But Barnaby couldn't possibly wait until tomorrow.

He had a lot of work to do.

Barnaby painted all morning, all afternoon, and into the evening.

As the sun set, Barnaby painted the finishing touches.

Barnaby ran into the house.
"Come see my tree house," said Barnaby. "I just finished painting it."
"It's too dark outside," said Barnaby's father. "We'll see it first thing in the morning."
"Can I have a tree house party tomorrow?" asked Barnaby.
"Sure," said Barnaby's mother.

That evening Barnaby called his friends to invite them to the tree house party.

While Barnaby's mother made pitchers of cherry punch and baked sugar cookies with sprinkles, Barnaby's father helped blow up balloons.

That night Barnaby and Baxter heard rumbling thunder and saw streaks of lightning. Then rain poured down on Blackberry Lane.
"I hope the rain stops by tomorrow," said Barnaby, "or my party will be ruined."

By morning the rain had stopped and the sun was shining.
The air was crisp and clear.
It was the perfect day for a tree house party.

Barnaby and Baxter hopped down the stairs and skipped out the door. They couldn't believe what they saw.

Barnaby raced inside
and sprinted up the stairs.

"All the paint has washed away," cried Barnaby.

Then Barnaby and his father hopped aboard their boat and sailed swiftly to town.

Barnaby and his father arrived at Hardy's Hardware Store.
"How can I help you today?" asked Mr. Hardy.
"We need lots of red paint — the kind that won't wash off in the rain," said Barnaby.
"And a bunch of brushes and some smocks, please," said his father.

Mr. Hardy mixed two gallons of Fire Engine Red,
Barnaby's favorite color.
Then he gave Barnaby a painting cap and a special brush.
"Happy painting," called Mr. Hardy.

When Barnaby arrived home, his friends were gathered under his tree house.
"I guess we're not having a tree house party," said Baisley.
"It's not a tree house party," said Barnaby.

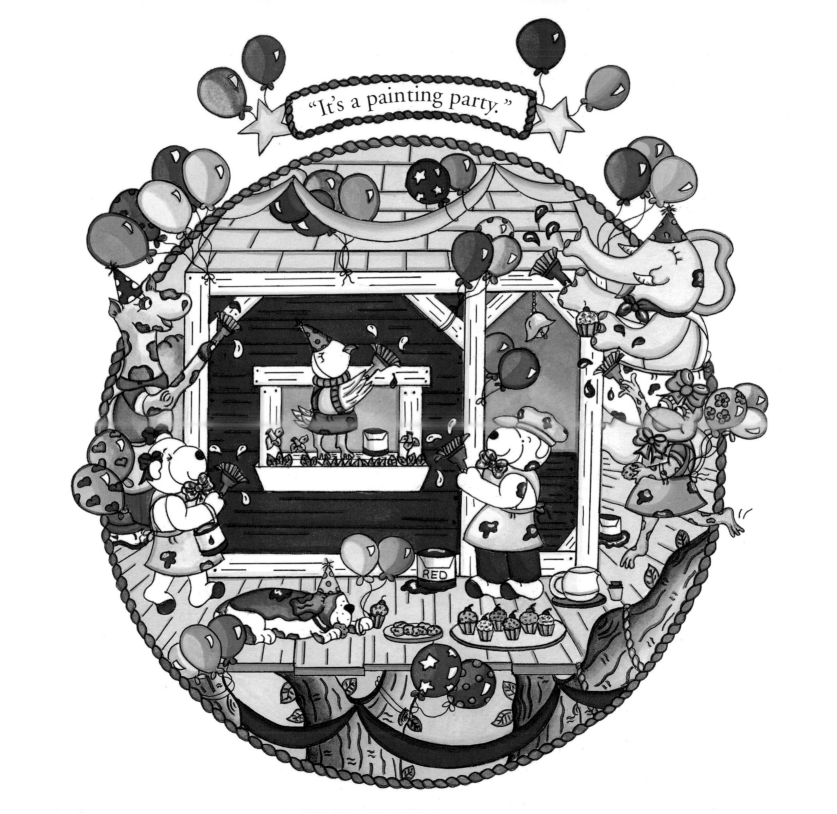